COUNTRY PROFILES

IRAQ

BY EMILY ROSE OACHS

BELLWETHER MEDIA • MINNEAPOLIS, MN

Blastoff! Discovery launches a new mission: reading to learn. Filled with facts and features, each book offers you an exciting new world to explore!

This edition first published in 2018 by Bellwether Media, Inc.

No part of this publication may be reproduced in whole or in part without written permission of the publisher.
For information regarding permission, write to Bellwether Media, Inc., Attention: Permissions Department,
5357 Penn Avenue South, Minneapolis, MN 55419.

Library of Congress Cataloging-in-Publication Data

Names: Oachs, Emily Rose, author.
Title: Iraq / by Emily Rose Oachs.
Description: Minneapolis, MN : Bellwether Media, Inc., 2018.
 | Series: Blastoff! Discovery: Country Profiles | Includes bibliographical references and index. | Audience: Grades 3-8.
 | Audience: Ages 7-13.
Identifiers: LCCN 2016057455 (print) |
   LCCN 2017003350 (ebook) | ISBN 9781626176829
   (hardcover : alk. paper) | ISBN 9781681034126 (ebook)
Subjects: LCSH: Iraq–Juvenile literature. | Iraq–Social life and customs–Juvenile literature.
Classification: LCC DS70.62 .O23 2018 (print) | LCC DS70.62 (ebook) | DDC 956.7–dc23
LC record available at https://lccn.loc.gov/2016057455

Text copyright © 2018 by Bellwether Media, Inc. BLASTOFF! DISCOVERY and associated logos are trademarks and/or registered trademarks of Bellwether Media, Inc. SCHOLASTIC, CHILDREN'S PRESS, and associated logos are trademarks and/or registered trademarks of Scholastic Inc., 557 Broadway, New York, NY 10012.

Editor: Christina Leaf   Designer: Brittany McIntosh

Printed in the United States of America, North Mankato, MN.

TABLE OF CONTENTS

IRAQ MUSEUM	4
LOCATION	6
LANDSCAPE AND CLIMATE	8
WILDLIFE	10
PEOPLE	12
COMMUNITIES	14
CUSTOMS	16
SCHOOL AND WORK	18
PLAY	20
FOOD	22
CELEBRATIONS	24
TIMELINE	26
IRAQ FACTS	28
GLOSSARY	30
TO LEARN MORE	31
INDEX	32

IRAQ MUSEUM

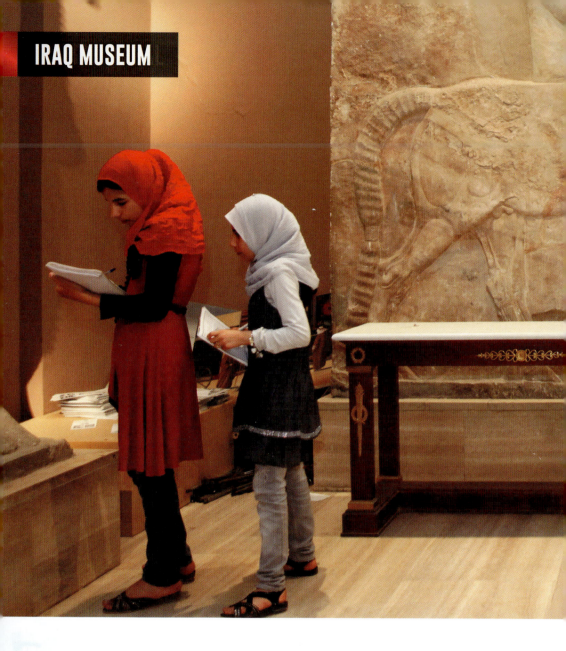

A school group walks into the grand building of the Iraq Museum in Baghdad. Inside, ancient **artifacts** from throughout Iraq's lengthy history and many **civilizations** surround the children. They spot Babylonian clay tablets with written text from more than 2,000 years ago. Elegant gold jewelry also stands on display.

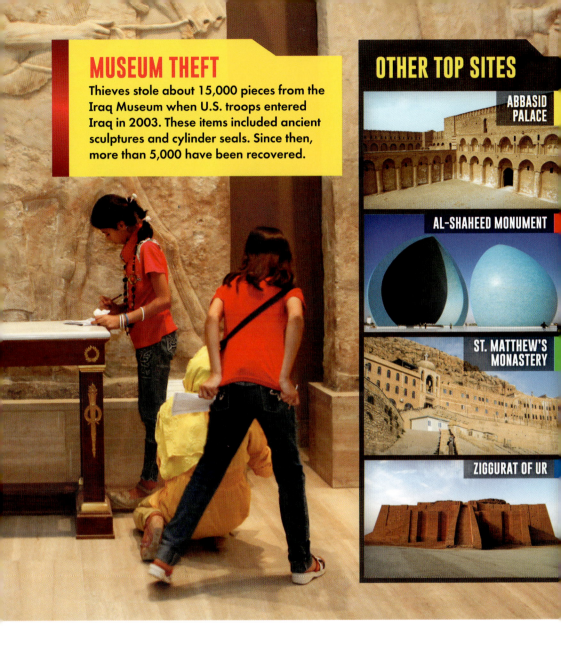

MUSEUM THEFT

Thieves stole about 15,000 pieces from the Iraq Museum when U.S. troops entered Iraq in 2003. These items included ancient sculptures and cylinder seals. Since then, more than 5,000 have been recovered.

OTHER TOP SITES

ABBASID PALACE

AL-SHAHEED MONUMENT

ST. MATTHEW'S MONASTERY

ZIGGURAT OF UR

The students admire massive Assyrian panels of carved stone showing images of battles, hunts, and guards. Then they head upstairs. There, they find beautiful **mosaics** created by ancient Sumerians. They date back thousands of years to the first civilization. These are just some of the wonders that Iraq holds!

LOCATION

Iraq is an **Arab** country in southwestern Asia. It is part of a region known as the **Middle East**. The country covers 169,235 square miles (438,317 square kilometers). Iraq's capital, Baghdad, lies near the center of the country.

Iran makes up Iraq's eastern border. To the north sit Turkey and Syria. Jordan is Iraq's western neighbor. Saudi Arabia and Kuwait lie to the south. For just 36 miles (58 kilometers), southeastern Iraq borders the Persian **Gulf**.

LANDSCAPE AND CLIMATE

= MESOPOTAMIA

Deserts fill the landscape of much of southern and western Iraq. In the northeast, mountains rise along Iraq's borders with Iran and Turkey. The Tigris and Euphrates Rivers flow across central Iraq. The **fertile** plains between them are called Mesopotamia. In the southeast, the rivers join and empty into the Persian Gulf. Broad, rolling **plains** cover most of eastern Iraq.

NINEVEH GOVERNORATE

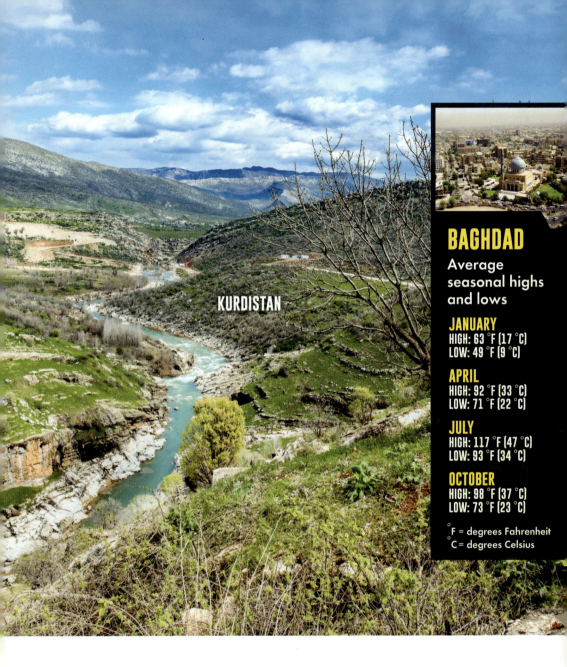

KURDISTAN

BAGHDAD
Average seasonal highs and lows

JANUARY
HIGH: 63 °F (17 °C)
LOW: 49 °F (9 °C)

APRIL
HIGH: 92 °F (33 °C)
LOW: 71 °F (22 °C)

JULY
HIGH: 117 °F (47 °C)
LOW: 93 °F (34 °C)

OCTOBER
HIGH: 98 °F (37 °C)
LOW: 73 °F (23 °C)

°F = degrees Fahrenheit
°C = degrees Celsius

Iraq mostly sees hot, dry summers. Winters tend to be mild with some rain. The cold northern mountains occasionally receive heavy snow. In the spring, this melting snow may flood Iraq's rivers and plains.

WILDLIFE

The chukar partridge is Iraq's national bird. In the northeast mountains, these birds search for plants or insects to eat. Jackals and hyenas roam along the Tigris and Euphrates Rivers. Carp and smooth-coated otters swim in these rivers' waters.

Iraq's deserts are home to sand cats. These small cats hunt even smaller animals, such as jerboas and gerbils. **Venomous** Arabian horned vipers hide beneath desert sands to surprise and capture lizards and birds.

CHUKAR PARTRIDGE

STRIPED HYENA

SMOOTH-COATED OTTER

ARABIAN HORNED VIPER

GOLDEN JACKAL

SAND CAT

SAND CAT

Life Span: 13 years
Red List Status: least concern

sand cat range =

| LEAST CONCERN | NEAR THREATENED | VULNERABLE | ENDANGERED | CRITICALLY ENDANGERED | EXTINCT IN THE WILD | EXTINCT |

PEOPLE

More than 38 million people call Iraq home. Two main groups of people make up the country's population. Most Iraqis are Arabs, while a smaller number are Kurds. The Kurds live in a northeastern region called Kurdistan and speak Kurdish. Arabs live throughout the rest of Iraq. They most often speak Arabic. Both Arabic and Kurdish are official languages of Iraq.

Almost all Iraqis practice Islam. They are divided into two Muslim groups, the Sunni and Shi'ite. There are about twice as many Shi'ites as Sunnis. Very few Christians, Hindus, Buddhists, and Jewish people live in Iraq.

FAMOUS FACE
Name: Zaha Hadid
Birthday: October 31, 1950
Hometown: Baghdad, Iraq
Famous for: Award-winning international architect who designed world-famous buildings in Germany, China, Italy, and Qatar

SPEAK ARABIC
Arabic uses script instead of letters. However, Arabic words can be written with the English alphabet so you can read them.

ENGLISH	ARABIC	HOW TO SAY IT
hello	marhaban	mar-HAB-ah
goodbye	ma'a as-salama	ma ahs-sah-LAH-mah
please (to males)	min fadlak	min FAHD-lehck
please (to females)	min fadlik	min FAHD-lick
thank you	shukran	SHUH-krahn
yes	na'am	NAHM
no	laa	LAH-ah

COMMUNITIES

Family holds an important place in Iraqi society. Often, Iraqis feel greater loyalty toward their families and tribes than their nation. Multiple generations of a family may live together. Even if they do not, relatives frequently visit each other. Adult children usually care for their elderly parents.

Most Iraqis live in cities, such as Baghdad. Apartments are common homes within cities. Houses in northern villages are usually made of stone. They may be built of mud and brick throughout the rest of the country. Roads, airplanes, and trains connect Iraq's cities to one another and to nearby countries.

BAGHDAD

CUSTOMS

Religion plays a very important role in the lives of many Iraqis. Five times a day, **muezzins** call out from **mosques** to remind Muslims that it is time to pray. Muslim men go to mosque each Friday to worship. Iraqis are expected to treat elders with respect. Often, they will not make eye contact when speaking with elders to show this respect.

HOLDING HANDS
In Iraq, male Arab friends sometimes hold hands with each other. This shows their close friendship and respect for each other.

HIJABS

Since the **Iraq War**, Iraqis have picked up some Western customs. They commonly dress in clothes similar to Americans and Europeans. Still, **traditional** Muslim women often choose to wear headscarves called *hijabs*.

17

SCHOOL AND WORK

Iraqi children must attend school from ages 6 to 12. After, students may go to intermediate school, followed by secondary school. In secondary school, students receive job training or continue their general studies. After graduation, some go on to university. Past wars have affected education in Iraq. However, it has been improving again in recent years.

Oil is Iraq's most important **export**. The oil industry employs many Iraqis. However, most hold **service jobs**. They may work in banks or for the government. Farmers near the Tigris and Euphrates Rivers produce barley, dates, and rice.

HARVESTING DATES

OIL PRODUCTION
Iraq is among the world's largest oil producers. In February 2017, it produced 4.57 million barrels a day!

OIL WORKER

PLAY

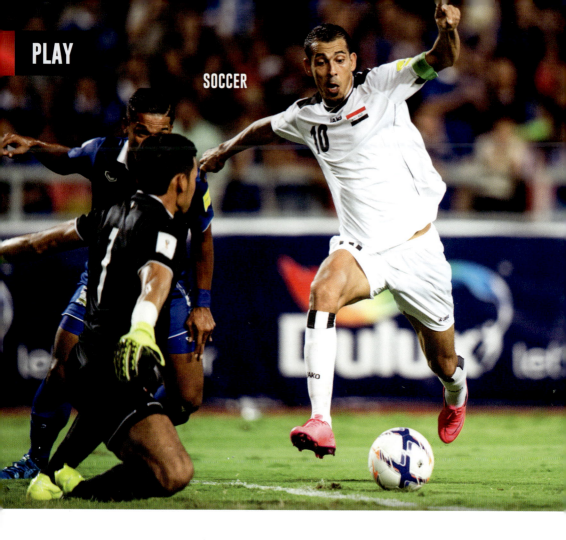

SOCCER

Soccer is Iraq's most popular sport. Kids love to play with friends or neighbors. Iraqis also cheer on their favorite teams from the sidelines or while watching on television. Basketball, boxing, horse racing, and tennis are also popular sports in Iraq.

BASKETBALL

Iraqi women enjoy sewing and watching television in their spare time. Men often meet in coffee shops to play games such as backgammon, dominoes, or chess.

Iraqis also enjoy dancing the *dabke*. This traditional dance is common at weddings. A ring of men holding hands dances to music from a drummer and flute player.

DOMINOES

CYLINDER SEAL ACTIVITY

In ancient Mesopotamia, Sumerians used cylinder seals to make documents official. These worked like signatures on important documents.

What You Need:
- air-drying clay
- unfolded paperclip
- stamp pad, any color

Instructions:
1. Tear off a large chunk of the air-drying clay. Roll it between your hands to form a cylinder that has ends about the size of a quarter. Make sure that the cylinder is about the same width throughout.
2. Cut off the ends of the cylinder to make it about 2 to 3 inches (5 to 8 centimeters) long.
3. Take the paperclip and carve designs into the soft clay. Once done, set it aside to dry. It may take a few days.
4. Once dry, roll the cylinder over the stamp pad. Press and roll the cylinder onto a sheet of paper. Now you have your very own cylinder seal!

FOOD

RIGHT HAND

Iraqis use only their right hands to eat, drink, and pass food. They consider using the left hand to be rude and unclean.

Lunch is the largest, most important meal of the day for Iraqis. Breakfast and dinner tend to be light meals. After a meal, Iraqis often eat dates and drink tea or coffee. The Islam religion does not allow Muslims to eat pork.

A flatbread called *khubz* is a **staple** in Iraqi diets. It may appear at every meal alongside dips and spreads. Rice with a stew of vegetables and lamb is a common meal. Other favorite foods include *kebabs*, or meat grilled on sticks, and rice-stuffed grape leaves called *dolmas*. *Masgouf* is a popular dish of grilled carp.

DOLMAS

MASGOUF

PISTACHIO DATE BALLS RECIPE

Ingredients:
1 cup dates, no pits

1 cup pistachios, shelled

1/4 cup ground pistachios

Steps:
1. With an adult present, put the dates into a food processor. Mix the dates until they form a paste.

2. Add the cup of pistachios to the date paste. Pulse until the pistachios are coarsely ground.
3. Scoop out the mixture. Roll it into 12 equal-sized balls. They should be sticky.
4. Place the ground pistachios in a small dish. Roll each ball in the dish to coat it with the ground pistachios.

CELEBRATIONS

Many of Iraq's biggest celebrations are Islamic holidays. A major holiday is Ramadan, a month of **fasting** and prayer. Muslims may eat only before sunrise and after sunset during this time. It ends with a three-day festival called *Eid al-Fitr*. Families dress in new clothing and celebrate with prayer, feasts, and gifts.

Eid al-Adha is another important holiday for Muslims. They attend mosque and visit graves of loved ones. They also give food to the poor and cook a feast for themselves. It is important to Iraqis that they honor their religion.

EID AL-ADHA

LIBERATION DAY

Iraqis celebrate Liberation Day on April 9. It marks the day that Iraq's cruel leader, Saddam Hussein, fell from power in 2003.

EID AL-FITR

TIMELINE

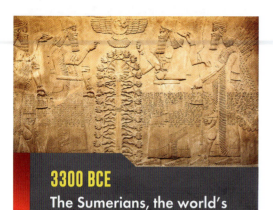

3300 BCE
The Sumerians, the world's first civilization, develop writing in Mesopotamia

762 CE
Abbasid rulers begin construction on a new city named Baghdad

637 CE
Islam and the Arabic language come to Iraq when Arabs gain control of the region

1258
Mongols attack Baghdad and the Abbasid rulers fall

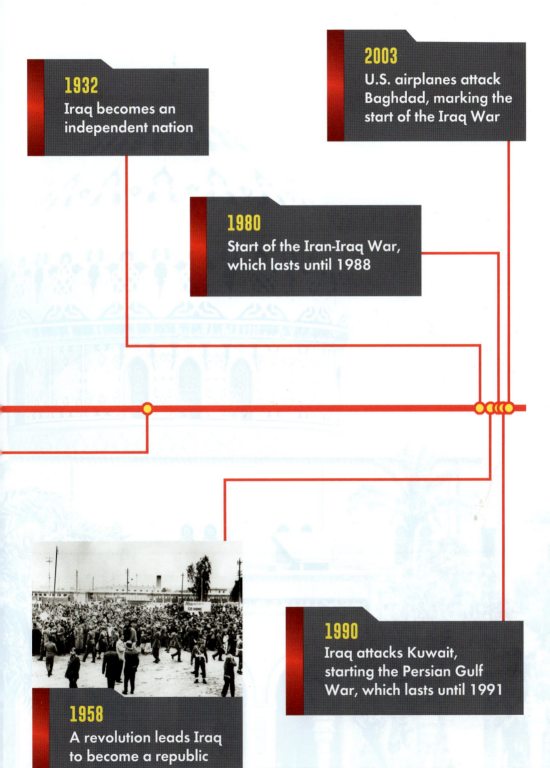

IRAQ FACTS

Official Name: Republic of Iraq

Flag of Iraq: Iraq's flag has three horizontal bands of color. The black bottom stripe is a symbol for the suffering Iraqis have faced. The red stripe on top stands for the blood lost while overcoming the suffering. In the middle, the white stripe represents the hope for a successful future. On it, green text reads, "*Allahu akbar,*" meaning "God is great." Iraq adopted its flag in 2008.

Area: 169,235 square miles (438,317 square kilometers)

Capital City: Baghdad

Important Cities: Mosul, Erbil, Basra

Population: 38,146,025 (2016 estimate)

WHERE PEOPLE LIVE
COUNTRYSIDE 30.5%
CITY 69.5%